A ZOMBIE VACATION

By Lisa Rose

Illustrated by Ángeles Ruiz

APPLES & HONEY PRESS

To my cousin/sister Michele
—LR

With all my love to Maria, my little daughter.
Thank you for your advice about how to paint zombies.
—ÁR

Apples & Honey Press
An imprint of Behrman House Publishers
Millburn, New Jersey 07041
www.applesandhoneypress.com

ISBN 978-1-68115-557-9

Library of Congress Cataloging-in-Publication Data

Names: Rose, Lisa, author. | Ruiz, Ángeles, 1971- illustrator.
Title: Zombie vacation / by Lisa Rose ; illustrated by Ángeles Ruiz.
Description: Millburn, New Jersey : Apples & Honey Press, an imprint of
Behrman House Publishers, [2020] | Summary: A zombie who has stopped being
frightening travels the world but finally finds that the Dead Sea is the
perfect place to relax. Includes facts about the Dead Sea and Israel.
Identifiers: LCCN 2019016621 | ISBN 9781681155579
Subjects: | CYAC: Zombies--Fiction. | Vacations—Fiction. | Dead Sea (Israel
and Jordan)—Fiction. | Israel—Fiction.
Classification: LCC PZ7.1.R6695 Zom 2020 | DDC [E]—dc23
LC record available at https://lccn.loc.gov/2019016621

Design by Elynn Cohen
Edited by Dena Neusner
Art directed by Ann D. Koffsky
Printed in China

1 3 5 7 9 8 6 4 2

072128.5K1/B1631/A8

The zombie in this book explores real places in Israel; p. 3, the shuk, a marketplace in
Jerusalem; p. 10, Sea of Galilee; p. 11, the Israel Museum, Jerusalem; p. 12, Luna Park,
Tel Aviv; pp. 20-21, the Dead Sea; pp. 22-23, Ein Gedi Nature Reserve. The zombie
also visits real places around the world: p. 14, Transylvania, Romania; p. 15 (top),
Mammoth Cave National Park, Kentucky; p. 15 (bottom), Bodie, California.

I felt tired.
My walk lacked the proper stiffness.

I had lost the urge to moan.
My skin no longer had its lovely dull, sickly color.
I wasn't scary anymore.

Little humans invited me to tea.

And big humans asked for my help.

Even cute tiny creatures were no
longer afraid of me.
I feared I would never scare
anyone again.

Being a zombie was hard work.
I thought I should take some
time to relax.

I tried massage,

yoga,

and even ballet.

But I *still* didn't feel like
stomping around with
my friends after dark.

Maybe I needed a vacation. There were lots of places to visit here in Israel.

I tried camping near the Sea of Galilee. But there were too many spectacular views.

The Israel Museum had too many beautiful things.

Luna Park in Tel Aviv had too many happy people.

It made me want to
go back to bed.

So I checked out popular monster spots around the world. Transylvania was too crowded with vampires.

Mammoth Cave was all booked
up with a bat family reunion.

In the ghost town of Bodie I kept running into spirits.

On my way back home,
I thought I would never moan again.

Until I saw this. . . .

The Dead Sea!

It was the perfect place for a zombie vacation.

At first, I saw a glorious hotel.

Bummer!

Then I noticed the old tattered hotel nearby,
with lots of zombies stalking around.

Hurray!

The hotel was crumbling into a sinkhole.
Roaches roamed the lobby.
My bed was bursting with bedbugs,
and there was a giant deathstalker
scorpion in my shower!

It was **perfect!**

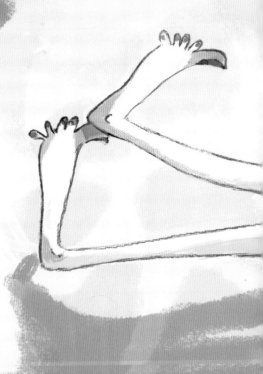

Next, I went to the beach.

I swam in the Dead Sea.
The salt made me float so much my hair stayed dry.
Not that I care about ruining my hairdo. It's already
perfectly messy!

The
UNDEAD
TIMES

DEAD SEA
Named top
vacation spot

Then, to get my zombie
groove back, I went hiking.

I saw a mountain gazelle, an Arabian leopard, and Egyptian vultures.

These endangered species were almost dead, like me.

Later, I gave myself a facial. It was so good for my skin. I was eight hundred years old and didn't look a day over six hundred!

And just when I thought it couldn't get any better, I danced to haunting organ music. I found a terrifying partner.

We even won the nightly creature
karaoke contest.

Finally, I was ready to return home.
I felt like myself again!

Well, almost myself.

THERE IS NO PLACE IN THE WORLD LIKE THE DEAD SEA.

You must come and visit. But hurry!
The Dead Sea is shrinking!

WHY IS THE DEAD SEA SHRINKING?

Israel is a desert. To live in this dry place, people needed fresh water. So pumping stations were created that diverted fresh water away from the Jordan River, which fed into the Dead Sea. The increase of fresh water helped farms and cities grow all around Israel. But this lack of fresh water caused the Dead Sea to evaporate more quickly. This also caused dangerous sinkholes. They can appear without warning and can take down roads, buildings, and beaches. In the past two decades, more than six thousand sinkholes have appeared all around the Dead Sea. Many areas are unsafe. The Ein Gedi beach shown in this book and other beaches have had to close.

WHAT LIVES IN THE DEAD SEA?

Plants and animals cannot live in the Dead Sea because of the high salt content. Only microorganisms such as bacteria and algae can live in these salty waters.

CAN YOU SWIM IN THE DEAD SEA?

Swimming in the Dead Sea is hard because it has a lot of salt in it, and salt water is heavier (denser) than fresh water. That makes it very difficult to dive under the water or swim any strokes. But it's *really* easy to float in the Dead Sea. The salt helps keep people on the surface of the water.

WHAT ABOUT ZOMBIES?

Zombies aren't real, but the *idea* of zombies comes from the folktales of a real place: the island nation of Haiti. Many traditions include imaginary beings. Jewish tradition has dybbuks, golems, and even demons. Some of these creatures might seem scary, but they're often used in books to get across a strong point or make the story more fun for you, the reader!

If you visit Israel, you can see the Dead Sea, as well as beautiful beaches, vast deserts, modern cities, holy sites, and the remains of cities from more than two thousand years ago. But you won't see any zombies!